COCK ROBIN

Illustrated by Barbara Cooney

Charles Scribner's Sons · New York

The Courtship,

Merry Marriage, and Feast of

COCK ROBIN

and Jenny Wren,

to which is added the Doleful Death of Cock Robin

The Courtship,

Merry Marriage, and Feast

of Cock Robin and Jenny Wren

It was a merry time
When Jenny Wren was young.
So neatly as she danced,
And so sweetly as she sung,
Robin Redbreast lost his heart—
He was a gallant bird—
He doft his hat to Jenny
And thus to her he said:

"My dearest Jenny Wren,
If you will but be mine,
You shall dine on cherry pie
And drink nice currant wine.
I'll dress you like a Goldfinch
Or like a Peacock gay.
So if you'll have me, Jenny,
Let us appoint the day."

Jenny blushed behind her fan
And thus declared her mind:
"Then let it be tomorrow, Rob,
I take your offer kind.
Cherry pie is very good!
So is currant wine!
But I will wear my russet gown
And never dress too fine."

Robin rose up early,
At the break of day.
He flew to Jenny Wren's house
To sing a roundelay.
He met the Cock and Hen
And bid the Cock declare
This was his wedding day
With Jenny Wren the fair.

The Cock then blew his horn
To let the neighbors know
This was Robin's wedding day
And they might see the show.
And first came Parson Rook
With his spectacles and band;
And one of Mother Hubbard's books
He held within his hand.

Then followed him the Lark,
For he could sweetly sing
And he was to be Clerk
At Cock Robin's wedding.
He sang of Robin's love
For little Jenny Wren.
And when he came unto the end,
Then he began again.

Then came the bride and bridegroom.
Quite plainly was she dressed,
And blushed so much, her cheeks were
As red as Robin's breast.
But Robin cheered her up—
"My pretty Jen," said he,
"We're going to be married
And happy then we'll be."

The Goldfinch came on next
To give away the bride.
The Linnet, being bridesmaid,
Walked by Jenny's side.
And as she was a-walking,
She said, "Upon my word,
I think that your Cock Robin
Is a very pretty bird."

The Bullfinch walked by Robin,
And thus to him did say,
"Pray, mark, friend Robin Redbreast,
That Goldfinch dressed so gay.
What though her gay apparel
Becomes her very well,
Yet Jenny's modest dress and look
Must bear away the bell."

The Blackbird and the Thrush,
And charming Nightingale,
Whose sweet jug sweetly echoes
Through every grove and dale,
The Sparrow and Tom Tit,
And many more were there.
All came to see the wedding
Of Jenny Wren the fair.

"O then," says Parson Rook,
"Who gives this maid away?"
"I do," says the Goldfinch,
"And her fortune I will pay.
Here's a bag of grain of many sorts,
And other things beside—
Now happy be the bridegroom,
And happy be the bride!"

"And will you have her, Robin,
To be your wedded wife?"
"Yes, I will," says Robin,
"And love her all my life."
"And will you have him, Jenny,
Your husband now to be?"
"Yes, I will," says Jenny,
"And love him heartily."

Then on her finger fair
Cock Robin put the ring.
"You're married now," says Parson Rook,
While the Lark aloud did sing—
"Happy be the bridegroom,
And happy be the bride!
And may not man, nor bird, nor beast,
This happy pair divide."

The birds were asked to dine,
Not Jenny's friends alone,
But every pretty songster
That had Cock Robin known.
They had a cherry pie,
Besides some currant wine,
And every guest brought something,
That sumptuous they might dine.

Now they all sat or stood
To eat and to drink
And everyone said what
He happened to think.
They each took a bumper
And drank to the pair—
Cock Robin the bridegroom
And Jenny Wren the fair.

The dinner things removed,
They all began to sing,
And soon they made the place
Near a mile around to ring.
The concert it was fine,
And every bird tried
Who best could sing for Robin
And Jenny Wren the bride.

Then in came the Cuckoo
And he made a great rout.
He caught hold of Jenny
And pulled her about.
Cock Robin was angry
And so was the Sparrow,
Who fetched in a hurry
His bow and his arrow.

His aim then he took,
But he took it not right.
His skill was not good,
Or he shot in a fright.
For the Cuckoo he missed,
But Cock Robin he killed!
And all the birds mourned
That his blood was so spilled.

The Doleful Death

of Cock Robin

C.R.

Who killed Cock Robin?
"I," said the Sparrow,
"With my bow and arrow,
I killed Cock Robin."

Who saw him die?
"I," said the Fly,
"With my little eye,
I saw him die."

Who caught his blood?
"I," said the Fish,
"With my little dish,
I caught his blood."

Who'll make his shroud?
"I," said the Beetle,
"With my little needle,
I'll make his shroud."

Who'll be the parson?
"I," said the Rook,
"With my little book,
I'll be the parson."

Who'll dig his grave?
"I," said the Owl,
"With my spade and trowel,
I'll dig his grave."

Who'll be the clerk?
"I," said the Lark,
"If 'tis not in the dark,
I'll be the clerk."

Who'll carry his coffin?
"I," said the Kite,
"If it be in the night,
I'll carry his coffin."

Who'll be chief mourner?
"I," said the Dove,
"Because of my love,
I'll be chief mourner."

Who'll sing a psalm?
"I," said the Thrush,
As she sat in a bush,
"I'll sing a psalm."

Who'll bear the pall?
"We," said the Wren,
Both the Cock and the Hen,
"We'll bear the pall."

Who'll toll the bell?
"I," said the Bull,
"Because I can pull."
And so Cock Robin farewell.

All the birds of the air
Fell to sighing and sobbing
When they heard the bell toll
For poor Cock Robin.